Libby
and the
Shooting
Star

Wish Foundation

By Julia Collins • Art by George Franco

SWEETBAY PRESS

6/18

Libby and the Shooting Star Wish Foundation
Text copyright © 2018 Julia Collins
Illustrations copyright © 2018 George Franco
Book design by Julia Collins

Collins, Julia.
Libby and the Shooting Star Wish Foundation; illustrated by George Franco.
pages cm

Summary: When Mary's little lamb wishes upon a star, she sets off to school
to learn how to make her wish, and those of others, come true.

ISBN 978-0-692-05293-8
[1. Science & Technology—Juvenile Fiction
2. Social Issues (Friendship) — Juvenile Fiction
3. School & Education—Juvenile Fiction]

The author is available by request for special reading and STEM events.
For details visit libbyandtheshootingstar.com

First Edition

SweetBay Press

For J.P.K.—grandfather, renaissance man, and rocket scientist.
And for my mother and favorite teacher of all,
Susan King Boyle.

Mary had a little lamb. Her name was Libby Snow.
Libby lived on a farm with an old horse, a pig, a shaggy dog, and a cat.

Every night, Libby looked up from the pasture at the sky, waiting for a shooting star.

Each time she saw one,
her wish was the same.

"I wish I could travel into outer space,"
Libby would say. "I want to know
what's up there."

One night, as Libby caught the glimpse of a star's silver tail, she made her wish.
The old horse overheard her.
"Why don't you follow Mary to school one day? Then you could learn how to
travel into outer space for yourself," he said.
"Really?" Libby said. "I didn't know I could go to school. I'm just a farm animal."

Despite her doubts, Libby's curiosity got the best of her.
The very next morning, Libby awoke early, waited for Mary to leave,
and began following quietly behind her.

When Libby arrived at school and took a seat at an empty desk, all the children laughed at her.

HAHA!

HAHA!

"What are you doing here? You're a sheep!" They laughed. "You should be back at the barn."

"I wish to learn," Libby said timidly.

The teacher quieted the other children and welcomed Libby to the class.

Every day thereafter, Libby followed Mary to school.

While the other children laughed and played, Libby studied. In addition to reading, she learned science, technology, engineering, and math. She learned about astronauts and rocket ships, planets and stars.

Every night, Libby planned her trip into outer space.

She was building a

rocket ship.

Finally, the day came for Libby to fly her rocket ship. She strapped herself in tight, started the engine, and began her countdown.

The rocket rumbled and rose slowly. Then suddenly, it shot off into the sky, past the houses, past the trees, past the clouds, all the way into outer space.

"I did it! I did it!" she said proudly. "I'm in outer space!"

As she looked all around in wonder, Libby saw the glow of a star shooting across the sky, much closer than ever before. Steering her rocket ship toward it, she took out a net and set off to catch it.

SWIPE!

The net cradled the star, and Libby brought it into her hands.
To her surprise, the star was engraved with hundreds of words.

"Why, these are wishes!" said Libby in astonishment.

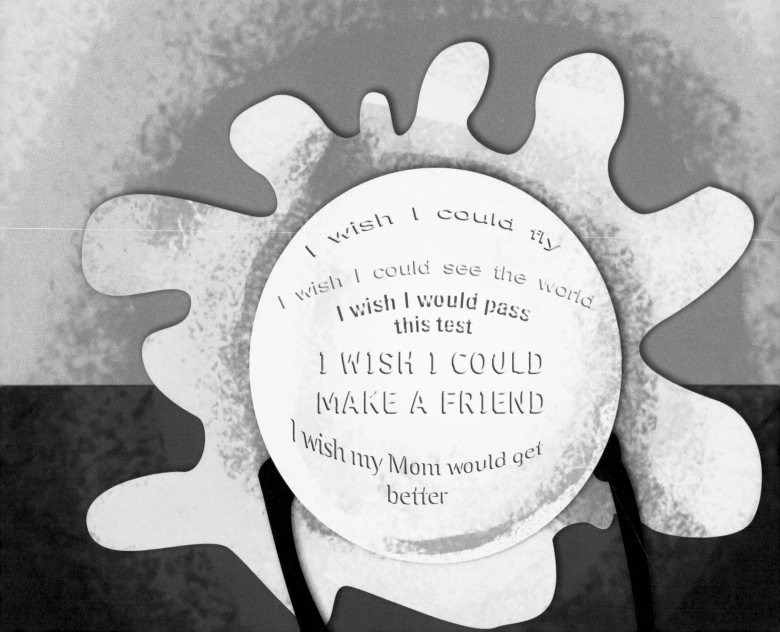

I wish I could fly

I wish I could see the world

I wish I would pass this test

I WISH I COULD MAKE A FRIEND

I wish my Mom would get better

"I wish I could make these wishes come true," she thought.

Then, an idea began to take shape in her mind. "I will! I will help these wishes come true," she said, full of excitement.

Clutching the star tight, Libby turned her rocket ship around and headed back to Earth.

When she returned home, she ran straight to school and whispered her plan to her teacher.

"What a wonderful idea, Libby!" teacher said. "What would you like to call it?"

"The Shooting Star Wish Foundation," Libby replied. "With the right tools and the right attitude, anyone can achieve their dreams. And I'm going to help them."

"Star, could you please take me to the makers of these wishes?" she asked.

The star began to shutter and shake. It began to roll slowly across the room and stopped right under the desk of Little Miss Muffet.

Libby walked over. "Miss Muffet, did you wish on a shooting star?" she asked.

"Yes. I did," Miss Muffet replied shyly. "I wish... I wish... I wish Spider would stop frightening me."

"Hmm. Let's think about this another way," Libby said. "Have you ever thought that he might not be trying to frighten you? That he might just want to be your friend? Have you tried saying hello?"

"No. I never thought of that. He's too scary looking," Miss Muffet replied.

"Let's try together. Sometimes it's easier to do things that frighten you when you have a friend by your side," Libby said.

Libby and Miss Muffet approached Spider on the playground.

"Hi Spider. Would you like to play tag with us?"
"Sure! I'd love to," Spider replied. "You're it!"

As the three of them took off running, a new friendship was born.

Two wishes had been granted that day. The
Shooting Star Wish Foundation was off to a great start.

The End

Acknowledgements

This book—which I hope will inspire in young children an excitement for learning and STEM, and encourage them to extend kindness to others—came together so naturally thanks to the guidance and support of many friends and colleagues.

Thank you to my daughter, Kingsley Jane, for insisting I read two books, tell two stories, and sing two songs every night, without which this story would never have been imagined. To my husband, who has supported me wholeheartedly throughout this endeavor. To Dawn for helping me learn to live my best life. To Amanda, my sounding board, who helped me (finally) come up with an ending. To Sarah, a true friend and cheerleader. To Deb, my editor. To Susanna, my selfless web designer. To George, who brought my story to life. And to countless others who provided feedback and support along the way.

CPSIA information can be obtained
at www.ICGtesting.com
Printed in the USA
BVHW05n1757220318
510932BV00001B/2/P